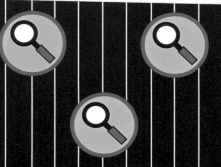

MW00834468

THE *mini* FIVE-MINUTE MYSTERIES

BY KEN WEBER

RUNNING PRESS
PHILADELPHIA · LONDON

A Running Press® Miniature Edition™
© 2004 K.J. Weber Limited
Front and back cover illustrations © DigitalVision/PictureQuest

Library of Congress Control Number: 2004110536

ISBN-13: 978-0-7624-2071-1
ISBN-10: 0-7624-2071-5

This book may be ordered by mail from the publisher. Please include $1.00 for
postage and handling. *But try your bookstore first!*

Running Press Book Publishers
125 South Twenty-second Street
Philadelphia, Pennsylvania 19103-4399

Visit us on the web!
www.runningpress.com

CONTENTS

INTRODUCTION

Mystery buffs are the only readers that get a kick out of winning *and* losing. They love beating an author to the punch by figuring things out before the end of the story. But they also love to be fooled! *Mini Five-Minute Mysteries* offers both possibilities for these are mysteries you are invited to solve. Most of the time you should be able to, but just in case we've included solutions. The magnifying glass symbols may help;

one means "not too hard";

two means you may have to sweat a bit, and so on. Above all, have fun!

If you *are* a mystery buff, then winning or losing doesn't really matter anyway!

A CLEAN PLACE TO MAKE AN END OF IT

What intrigued Bob Gibson—bothered him, actually—was how *clean* the inside of the car was. Someone, quite possibly the dead woman herself, had vacuumed the interior rugs with special care. There wasn't a speck of dust anywhere on the dash, either, or along the steering column; even the short stalks behind the knobs on the radio had been wiped. The leather cover over the gearshift box had been cleaned of the dust and grit that always collect in the creases. That had taken a wet cloth or a chamois, Bob realized. So the cleaning was not just a casual, spontaneous effort.

It wasn't a new car. From where he was leaning into it, with both fists pressed into the driver's seat, Bob peered a little closer at the odometer. The light wasn't all that good in the little garage, and the car had been backed in so that the waning winter daylight from the open garage door came through the windshield directly into his face. Still, he could make out the figures: 47,583. No, not a new car at all. But one in great shape.

Bob leaned across the seat and, with the tip of his index finger, ticked the switch to lower the passenger window just a bit. He checked to see if the earnest young policeman at the door had noticed, but he hadn't. If he had, and objected, Bob would have argued. The smell in the car was nauseating, and he needed to relieve it by letting a bit of draft through.

It was a smell he'd encountered before. Not so often as to be familiar with it. Maybe a half-dozen times or so in the past thirty years, but after the first time he'd never forgotten. It was the smell of a body in the early stages of decomposition;

a hint of sweet and a hint of foul. Sickening.

The smell clung, too. The garage door had been open for several hours, ever since the body had been discovered earlier, around noon. But the whole building was still filled with the odor, and Bob knew it would be a long time before the fabric in the car would be free of it.

Inside the car, of course, it was worse. The doors had been open only long enough for the photographer to do her grisly job, and then again when the coroner removed the body. Bob was there to tow away the car to the police pound.

Over his years as owner of Palgrave Motors, Bob had come to know the police very well and he was the one they invariably called in situations like this. Therefore it was not, as he had reflected only seconds before, the first time he had been called to the scene of a suicide. Nevertheless, although all he had to do was take away the car, the whole business gave him the creeps.

According to the coroner, the woman—Bob didn't know her name—had backed the car into the little garage some forty to fifty hours ago, closed the door and simply sat there with the motor running until the inevitable happened. The body had gone unnoticed for almost two days, the coroner estimated.

"You didn't touch anything, did you?"

It was Officer Shaw. Bob hadn't heard him come in. The young policeman had been left behind by the investigating detective with specific and stern instructions that nothing was to be disturbed. Shaw took the order seriously.

Bob looked at him, uncertain just how to put his suspicions. He pointed to the two-way radio in Shaw's belt.

"Can you call your sergeant on that?"

Shaw didn't answer; he just looked at Bob curiously.

"'Cause I think he'll want to take another look at all this," the older man said. "Missed something, I think."

Why has Bob Gibbon drawn this conclusion?

SOLUTION:

One of the very clear pieces of evidence is that the body has been dead for some time. The odor makes that certain, so it is quite likely that, as the coroner says, the victim has been dead for forty to fifty hours.

Therefore, if the woman backed the car into the garage that long ago, and left the motor running until she died, the car would have run out of fuel, and the battery would have been drained to powerlessness owing to the fact that the ignition was left on. Yet Bob was able to lower one of the windows by simply ticking the switch. He suspects that this car may not be the place where the person died.

Linc Dennebar had planned every step of the robbery with great care, but killing Mary Majeski turned out to be more of a problem than he had anticipated. Not actually doing it; he'd rehearsed that part so often in his mind, the real thing was almost automatic. Mary's late husband had been a judge, and she kept his gavel on the mantelpiece. Linc simply took it and, with one blow to the back of her head, he . . .

well, he knew from the way it felt that one swing was all that was needed. Exactly as he'd planned; she probably never even felt it. What he didn't expect; what he hadn't planned for, was the nausea, the wrench in his gut and the panic that overcame him when he looked at her lying so still on the floor in front of her wheelchair.

Later, when he was arrested, Linc realized it must have been the panic that led to his one big mistake. But at the time, when he called 9-1-1 on Mary's old rotary phone—the next step in his careful plan—the panic made him sound really genuine, even better than he'd practiced. Maybe too good, he thought. Might make the police get here faster, so it was a good thing he had the third step timed for speed.

That was to get the rings and bracelets into the hollow bottoms of his Nikes. He knew just which ones to take: Linc had learned all about heisting jewelry from an old con up at Rojax. That was the adult detention center where he'd done 180 days instead of at the juvenile house because some bleeding-heart social worker convinced the court that Rojax had the facilities to start him on a trade. He'd learned a trade all right: the old con had even taught him how to fix the shoes, explaining how high-tech basketball footwear was the best thing that had happened to B&E since pawn shops.

Next, after pulling open all the drawers in the roll-top desk, along with a few cupboard doors in the tiny kitchen, and then breaking a glass at the sink, Linc had called Mr. Peevey back at the drug store, telling him about the horrible scene he had just walked into. This part of the plan was something Linc had worked on very carefully.

For the past several years, long before Linc came on the scene, Mary had been getting her medications delivered from Mr. Peevey's pharmacy on Thursdays—Thursday afternoons. That was an important coincidence, because the people in two of the other apartments in the little brownstone were always at work then. Linc had taken awhile to confirm this after he had first seen Mary put the jewelry into the roll-top. As for the one remaining apartment, it was empty for the month, as the couple renting it was away on a summer vacation.

The other part of the Peevey Plan—he liked calling it that—was the delay strategy. Mr. Peevey knew how long it took to get to Mary Majeski's and back, but Linc had been stretching that a bit each time, telling Peevey that the old lady always seemed to have a bit of fetch and carry to ask of him when he showed up with her weekly package. The druggist didn't seem to mind that. She was a long-time, faithful customer, and good public behavior like that sure wouldn't harm the business if he ever needed to call attention to it.

Linc had wondered how he'd keep the call short—Mr. Peevey was a talker and would want all kinds of detail, but, again, being genuinely upset made it easy to just hang up.

After the call to his boss, there were still crucial things left to do. First, Linc pushed over a chair and jolted a knick-knack table off its accustomed site hard enough so that a cup and saucer fell to the rug. Yes, the rug. He almost forgot about that! Linc took a big, firm cushion and wiped out his Nike tracks, leaving those areas where they'd be reasonably expected.

Finally, he went out into the main hallway, closed the door, then forced it open with a screwdriver. This would be the final, clear indication of a B&E, the cap to his story: Linc Dennebar, delivery boy for Peevey's Pharmacy, arrives at Mary Majeski's apartment same as always; sees the open door; sees the old lady on the floor; calls the police. Straight and simple.

By now he could hear a siren—

then two. Linc sprinted to the back of the hallway, secretly blessing old buildings, and dropped the screwdriver down a cold air register. Moving quickly, for the sirens were coming from the street below now, he pulled off the surgical gloves he had been careful to wear the whole time, stuffed them down after the screwdriver, and sprinted back to the door. Here, he hesitated for several long and agonizing seconds. This was a part of the plan that he had never been able to finalize with confidence. Should he wait for the cops at the door? Too cool. Go to the top of the stairs and shout? They might shoot him! Run down the stairs to the street? A little too freaked out. Or should he stay in the apartment with old Mary? Might look loyal and concerned, but . . .

At the last second he opted for running down the stairs. It would look better, he figured. "Upstairs! Quick, quick!" he yelled.

What was Linc Dennebar's one big mistake?

SOLUTION:

Linc wore gloves throughout the affair so he wouldn't leave finger-prints. That means, however, that his prints are not on Mary's tele-phone, which he used to report the crime.

Out of habit, Vince Moro reached up to clean a fingerprint off the rearview mirror, before adjusting it down a bit so he could see out the back. Then he picked up the envelope that was balled up and stuffed behind the gearshift in the center console, and put it in the glove compartment.

Don't know why I'm doing this, Vince thought as he reached over to pick up a pair of cigarette butts from the floor on the passenger side. "I really don't know why." This time he had said it out loud, while throwing the two butts out the passenger side window, what was left of it.

The fact was, Vince was compulsively neat, and nothing bothered him more than a messy car. It was a point of personal pride that no vehicle left Vince's Auto Body dirty. Not ever, no matter how tiny or insignificant the repair.

But this car? There was surely no point in cleaning it. Certainly no point in trying to repair it. The thing was a write-off, and Vince was simply here to tow it away to the wrecking yard. The front and back of the car were okay. In fact, the dash had that spotless, uncluttered look Vince always liked in cars that had just left a rental agency. And the shelf beneath the back window was pleasantly free of the invariable accumulation of clutter and junk.

The front seats, however, and the front windows, the center post, even the roof above the front seat: they were a different matter. The killers had sprayed so many bullets over these areas that the headrest on the passenger seat had been chewed right off, leaving a frothy stump of stuffing, its original whiteness now covered in drying blood. A few minutes ago Vince had overheard one of the investigators—he was sure it was one of the CIA guys—say that both victims had taken over twenty rounds in the upper torso.

"You the guy from Hertz?"

The voice in Vince's ear startled him, but he strove not to show it. His hearing more than his sight told him it was the sergeant from the highway patrol. Although the two men had met before, more than once, the sergeant never, ever recognized Vince. Or pretended not to. Vince didn't like him.

"I have been *retained* by Hertz," Vince said, getting out of the car with deliberate slowness. "I'm here to take the car. It's cleared to go?"

He folded his arms and leaned against the car. It was the same sergeant all right. A tall fellow, at least a head taller than Vince. And he had the annoying habit of standing so close when he talked that the other person had to lean back to look up, or else step backward. That's why Vince leaned against the car.

"Not yet," the sergeant replied as he took off his hat and wiped his forehead with his sleeve. Vince was sure he was actually moving closer.

"Not yet," the policeman said again. "There has to be some—"

"Okay, Sergeant, if you will,

please! The photographer can use you now."

Vince whipped around quickly. It was not a voice he'd heard before, today or at any time. The accent was British, and as the speaker approached, Vince knew he was a complete stranger. That was not surprising; the place was crawling with investigators. The CIA was here; Vince knew that for sure. And the RCMP. Two of them had come from Ottawa in a Lear jet. And the whole scene had been shut down while they waited for two more people to come up from Buffalo. No one had told Vince directly, but he could tell they were in charge. Now who the British guy was, Vince had no idea at all, but certainly he was connected with the affair.

Just before dawn, two diplomats, from the French consulate in Buffalo, New York, had crossed into

Canada over the Rainbow Bridge at Niagara Falls. Not more than a few minutes later, while stopped at a traffic light, they were shot down in an absolute storm of machine-gun bullets. Then their bodies had been dragged out of the car and, as though to send a message, laid side by side in front of the car and sprayed with bullets again. The assassins had escaped.

"Excuse me, sir." The British

accent was very polite. A great deal more polite than the sergeant. "Who are . . . oh, yes. Forgive me!"

The man peered closer at the badge that dangled from Vince's shirt pocket and proclaimed CLEAR-ANCE—SITE ONLY.

"You're the gentleman here to tow away the vehicle, aren't you? If you don't mind waiting just a few minutes more. Some photos we need. It would be convenient if you didn't drive over the outlines there."

He pointed to the chalk outlines on the pavement in front of the car, which marked where the bodies of the diplomats had lain. The sergeant was now lying down beside the longer one. It was clear his dignity was wounded and Vince was just beginning to enjoy that when the accent said, "There's one more thing, actually. It's frightfully awkward, I know, but you . . . uh . . . you are just about the size of one of the victims. Do you . . . uh . . . would you mind awfully lying down there like the sergeant? I'm sorry, I can't really explain why, but it will help us. A reconstruct-the-scene sort of thing, you see."

For an instant, but only an instant, Vince wondered if maybe he wasn't being had. But the sergeant was already lying on the pavement, and the situation was hardly one for humor, macabre or otherwise. He nodded and went to the front of the car, glad now that he'd left on his coveralls to drive out here, and lay down beside the other outline.

"A bit embarrassing, this," Vince muttered to the sergeant. There was no response. The sergeant was definitely embarrassed and had no wish to discuss the fact. "All in the interests of justice," Vince continued, determined to make it known that he could make light of the indignity. "By the way," he said, "would it help if you knew which one of them was driving when they were shot?"

The sergeant sat bolt upright so suddenly that the photographer yelled. "How do you know?" the policeman asked.

How does Vince Moro know who was driving?

SOLUTION:

The two diplomats were of significantly different height. One was about the height of the sergeant, who is a head taller than Vince. The other was about Vince's height.

When Vince sat in the driver's seat of the car, waiting for clear-ance to tow it away he adjusted the rearview mirror *down* so he could see out the back. Therefore it must have been adjusted for a taller person before; the taller of the two diplomats.

TAGGERT'S TURF

P.C. Simpson Taggert was the oldest beat cop on the force. He may well have been the oldest beat cop in the entire country, but that didn't bother him in the least, for his life as a cop was just the way he wanted it. For Simpson Taggert, there were no politics; there was no sucking up to the brass, no pressure to fatten his personnel file. Best of all, he had his own turf. Sure, other cops took shifts on the same beat, for he couldn't be on duty twenty-four hours a day. But the others came and went. He stayed.

A few seconds ago, as he turned south off Prince Boulevard heading down Fawcett to number 41, Taggert had allowed himself a short, uncharacteristic smile when he realized that today was an anniversary—one that only he would remember, but that was just fine with him. Thirty-five years ago today, June 19, he'd turned down a promotion. There had been two more offers after that, both declined, and then they stopped. But with each offer he'd extracted a promise.

Taggert interrupted his reverie to pull over to the curb so he could look at the flowers in front of number 20. In many ways, Fawcett Avenue, like a lot of the residential streets around here, was a beat cop's dream. Quiet. Good people. Not big houses, but really well cared for. The lots were too small for professional landscaping, but every front yard had flowerbeds, and every backyard had a large, mature maple or elm, sometimes two or three. Number 20 he'd always called the "begonia house," for year after year the owners planted dark-leafed, red fibrous begonias. A bit boring to some, perhaps, but Taggert had learned enough from his wife to respect their choice.

"Morning sun for fibrous begonias," MaryKate would chant, "shade for your tuberous ones, and afternoon sun for your daisies." And he and MaryKate had planted that way every spring until the cancer took her.

It was because of MaryKate that he'd said no to the vice squad thirty-five years ago. They'd just bought a little house not unlike number 20, a fixer-upper that they wanted to work on together. Taggert was a good cop, and it wasn't hard to get the brass to agree to leaving him on the beat—his beat—the one he liked and came to know so well.

He pulled away from the curb before he started attracting attention. No use upsetting anyone at the start of the day with the sight of a police car in front of their house.

For the same reason he didn't stop at 41, just slowed enough to confirm the details in his memory bank: short sidewalk bisecting the small lot and running up to wide, wooden steps that led in turn to an old-fashioned verandah. Both sides of the steps were crowded by a pair of overgrown yews, with nicely maintained beds of periwinkle leading away to short cedar hedges that marked the limits of the property.

Taggert had been inside the house a few years before. Not a big deal. The husband, Trevor Banjee, was a pretty heavy drinker and had gotten drunk enough to frighten his wife into calling the station. By the time Taggert was able to respond, Banjee had passed out. He'd meant to come back the next day and read the riot act, but never got around to it. And Taggert had been there again only a month ago, just before he left on vacation. Part of a wider situation this time, a peeping Tom. There had been quite a number of 9-1-1 calls, several from Mrs. Banjee.

Fawcett ended in a cul-de-sac and Taggert made a U-turn to go back to Prince Boulevard. He didn't even glance at the "begonia house" this time. When he was upset, Taggert paid far less attention to his favorite spots, and he was particularly upset now. That young snippet at the coroner's office—she'd have to be told a thing or two about how to do proper investigations on his turf. Last week, the final week of Taggert's vacation, Mrs. Banjee had killed her husband, and that young whatever-her-name-was—he'd only met her once—had ruled it involuntary manslaughter.

At a red light, Taggert took the summary sheet from the file on the seat beside him.

"A beautiful sunny morning," it quoted Mrs. Banjee, I was out before the heat came. Trevor was still in bed—that's what I thought anyway; he usually is these days. And I was bent over, working on my ground-cover beds, my periwinkle, with the hand cultivator. Facing away from the street. And all of a sudden there was this shadow of someone right over me. So I swung! I mean, I was really scared! You know with that prowler around now, and it's always at dawn that he comes! Those prongs on the cultivator? They hit Trevor right on the side of the head, and he . . . [Subject too distraught to continue.]

Further along Prince Boulevard, Simpson Taggert turned into a Drive-Thru. He was hearing Mary-Kate again. "Never hurts to stop and have a cup of coffee before you jump into something. In the time it takes for the coffee to cool, you might just change your mind."

What Taggert thought the time might do was calm him down enough to approach the young woman at the coroner's office directly rather than go over her head. She was dead wrong—about the involuntary part, anyway—but then, as MaryKate would certainly have pointed out, he was young once, too, and made mistakes. Besides, he thought, it's probably better to have her onside if she's going to be working on Taggert's turf.

Why does Simpson Taggert disagree with the "involuntary" element in the killing of Mr. Banjee?

SOLUTION:

In the early morning, Simpson Taggert turns south on Fawcett Avenue. He pauses at 20 Fawcett to look at the fibrous begonias, which thrive on morning sun. Number 20 and all even numbered properties, therefore, must be on the west side of the street, which puts odd-numbered properties like number 41, the Banjee house, on the east side. In the early morning at the front of her house, therefore, Mrs. Banjee would not be suddenly surprised by a shadow, for the entire front would be in shadow. After noon, when the sun has moved into the south and toward the west, a shadow could be cast by someone approaching her porch, but not until then.

Mrs. Banjee was not frightened by a shadow as she says.

BRENHAM STUDIOS
PRODUCTION OFFICE

Harry,

This is what the kid Mallory
Hart came up with. It's
pretty good I kind of like it.
Lets the audience know right
up front what the Countess is
like. Lot cheaper too than the
big party scene Tilzer's got

planned for that. See what
you think. We'll have to
talk it over with Tilzer but
I say we shoot it no matter
what he wants. Especially
since the Venice set is still
up I checked this morning.
Shooting won't take more
than a couple hours.

Think budget!
KT

One thing: the kid thinks the scene should run <u>behind</u> the opening credits. I think it runs on its own, right after the "Venice Italy, 1502" opener. We can do credits at the end. ???

To: Korman Telfer
From: Mallory Hart

NEW OPENING SCENE—AS YOU
REQUESTED

After an establishing
shot of the Doge's palace
from across the canal,
the camera makes a slow
zoom to the balcony above
right of the front por-

tico. (This is the same
balcony where the Contessa
meets the French ambassa-
dor in Scene 12.) Double
doors are open. Camera
continues in and picks up
a cardinal standing on
one side of a small table.
Moves closer and shows the
Contessa standing on the
other side. She is gowned
and fully made up although

it is no later than midday. The cardinal is gussied up, too, but businesslike rather than churchy. Black cassock, not red. Red piping on it though, red sash, and the little red zuchetto on his head. Important he should look like someone who enjoys power more than holiness so that when she kills him there is probably some dark reason for it.

No dialogue in the scene that we can hear, but it's apparent the two have been talking, probably arguing. The camera has come in on a sort of intermission.

There is a silver decanter on the table, two silver goblets, a flat-bladed knife, also silver—not a weapon—and a reed basket full of apples. The Contessa pours wine into each of the two goblets, pushes one toward the cardinal, picks up the other, and takes a swallow. He doesn't touch his and gives her a "do-you-think-I'm-nuts?" look, so she sets hers down, pushes it toward him, and then takes his and drinks from it. He's impressed but still wary.

She's pouty now. Offended.
Offers the cardinal an
apple. He smiles. Doesn't
take it, and then uses both
hands to remove the top
layer of apples from the
basket. He picks an apple
from the bottom of the
basket and offers it to her.
This time it's the Contessa
who smiles. She accepts the

apple and moves to take
a bite but then suddenly
stops and nods respect-
fully, almost a bow. Like
she's forgotten her man-
ners. Sets the apple on
the table, spins it gently
a couple of times like a
top, and then cuts it in
half with the knife.

The Contessa picks up
one half of the apple and

takes a bite, looking at the cardinal. Without taking his eyes off her, he picks up the other half and bites into it, once, then twice, before a look of realization comes over his face, followed by a flash of anger before he falls. A couple of spasms and he's dead. She's still got her half

of the apple in her hand
and has another bite before
taking a step or two to
peer down at the now still
body of the cardinal.

Stays in this position
until fadeout. There is
a slight, bemused smile on
her face. Outside sounds
begin to come from the
canal. They hold through
the fade into Scene 1,

where the gondolas approach
the palace.

*In "the kid's" scene, the Contessa
manages to poison the cardinal. How?*

SOLUTION:

There was poison on one side of the knife blade, the side against the portion of apple the cardinal ate.

TO CATCH A MANNERLY THIEF

As she stepped over the potholes in the street and leaned hard into a fierce east wind, Agnes Skeehan made a promise to herself: never again was she going to attend a conference in November unless it was within walking distance of the equator. Actually, for Agnes, anywhere warmer than Liverpool would do. Liverpool may have produced the Beatles, and it could point with pride at its importance to the Industrial Revolution, but to Agnes that was hardly enough to make up for the miserable weather.

She mounted the curb, trotted across the sidewalk, and pulled hard at the entrance door of her hotel. Three days at the Birkenhead Arms had taught Agnes to yank with both hands at the ancient portal.

"Ah, young missy!" It was the hotel porter. He made a contribution all his own to Agnes's opinion of Liverpool. "You've got a tele-phone message here, young missy. All the way from Canada! A Deputy Commissioner Mowat. Sounds im-portant, missy. Talked to him myself, I did. Told him you were out, I did."

Agnes mumbled a thank you as she grabbed the message and ran for the creaky old elevator. As things stood at the moment, she was only three hours away from her flight home, but she had a feeling this call was going to change her schedule.

It did.

"I want you to stay over there in Liverpool and help them with this case," Deputy Commissioner Mowat's voice crackled and sputtered across the Atlantic only minutes later. "As a favor from us, you know, international police cooperation and all that." He paused, but then jumped in again as though to head off the objection he was expecting.

"You're simply the best there is on handwriting. They don't have anybody that comes close to you. Now what I want you to do right away is go to their headquarters—it's right by your hotel there—and report to Superintendent Anthony Opilis. He's the head of their CID: their Criminal Investigation Department. Now what I want you to do is consider yourself on temporary assignment there. Indefinite. As long as it takes."

Agnes struggled so hard to keep from telling Deputy Commissioner Mowat where he could stuff the international cooperation and the temporary assignment that she barely heard the rest. She didn't really need to though. The tabloids were full of the case that prompted his call. "The Friendly Filcher" one daily called it. "The Case of the Courteous Cat Burglar" another dubbed it. Whatever he—or she—

deserved to be called, the case involved an amazingly successful thief who was breaking into homes and stealing jewelry. He seemed to have a peculiar respect for his victims, and this, in addition to the size of the take, was what the papers found so interesting. At each theft—there had been seven now—the thief left behind a neatly handwritten note of apology and an assurance that the stolen pieces would find their way only into the hands of people who would appreciate their beauty and value.

These notes, Agnes knew, were the reason she was being loaned to the Liverpool CID. Mowat was right when he called her the best, Agnes Skeehan, *Corporal* Agnes Skeehan, fourteen-year veteran of the Royal Canadian Mounted Police, had a special interest and an even more special knack in handwriting analysis. At graduation from the police training college in Regina, circumstances had presented her with a choice of more study, or assignment to a mounted patrol at the Parliament Buildings in Ottawa. Since race-track-betting windows were as close to horses as Agnes ever cared to be, she picked the study and had never looked back. Eight months ago, her article in the *Journal of Forensic Science* had led to an invitation to address a conference in Liverpool. Little did she realize when she came down from the podium to a huge round of applause, that her next move would be, not to the airport, but into the superintendent's office at the Liverpool CID.

Superintendent Opilis, a long-time acquaintance of Deputy Commissioner Mowat as it turned out, was a plodder. His explanation of the jewelry thefts to Agnes was so detailed and so slow that she had to fight to pay attention. She kept turning her head toward the grimy office window to yawn, covering the move with a phony cough.

The superintendent must have sensed her mood for suddenly Agnes became aware of annoyance in his voice.

"Withenshawe?" he said, or rather, asked. "I say, Corporal Skeehan. You heard me? Withenshawe Purveyors?"

Agnes blushed. She had indeed been drifting. The problem was, she just didn't want to be in Liverpool.

"Yes, Superintendent, I'm sorry." She got up and walked to the window, trying to appear alert by focusing on a weathervane pointing at her from atop a pub across the street.

"Withenshawe Purveyors of Speke Street." She cleared her throat. "Every one of the notes was written on Withenshawe letterhead. I'm aware of that. And your people have definitely established that they were all written by the same left-handed person. I'm aware of that, too. But don't you think the Withenshawe Purveyors stationery is a most clumsy red herring? After all, who . . .

"Indeed, indeed Corporal Skeehan." Opilis got up and joined Agnes at the window. "But you see, there are other serious reasons why Alistair Withenshawe is a right handy suspect." He paused awkwardly. "We . . . er . . . we've summoned him. His office is just a short walk south of here. What we want you to do is . . . Why! That's him! Right there. Across the street."

"Him?" Agnes pointed at a tall, very nattily dressed gentleman holding down a bowler hat. "The dude with the hat? And the cane?

Look at him!" Agnes was fully awake now. "Does he always walk like that in public?"

"Yes, well," Superintendent Opilis was almost apologetic. "Ah, we have dealt with him before. I'm afraid he's a bit of a showman."

To prove the policeman's point, Alistair Withenshawe, who had been bouncing his cane off the edge of the curb and catching it, now began to twirl it high in the air like a drum major, spinning it first over one parked car, then the next, and then a third, before he brought it down and made a crisp military turn off the walk and into the street toward the police station.

Opilis let a touch of admiration creep into his voice. "Snappy, what?"

Agnes looked at him. "Yes, I agree. Snappy. But I'll give you any odds you want he didn't write those notes."

Why is Agnes Skeehan so sure of that?

SOLUTION:

Agnes Skeehan walks into her hotel leaning into a strong east wind. She responds to Deputy Commissioner Mowat's phone call and he tells her to go right to the office of the Liverpool CID, specifically to Superintendent

Opilis. Through the window of the superintendent's office Agnes notices a weathervane on a pub across the street pointing right at her. Since the wind is from the east (blowing *toward* the west) the superintendent's office must therefore be on the east side of a street that runs north-south.

Both Agnes and the superintendent then see Alistair Withenshawe across the street, walking to the police station because he was summoned there. Opilis told

Agnes that Withenshawe Purveyors has an office just a short walk to the south. Therefore, this "dude" as Agnes called him, is walking toward the north, on the west side of the street. His cane must be in his street-side hand, or *right* hand, for he first bounces it off the curb, then twirls it over parked cars.

Agnes concludes that to engage in such adept cane work, Alistair Withenshawe must be using his preferred hand, his right hand, the same hand he would use to write notes. Since the jewel thief's notes are written by a left-handed person, Agnes is willing to give odds that Withenshawe didn't write them.

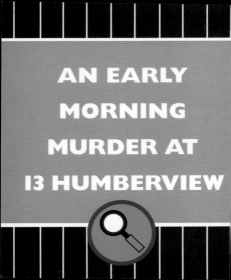

Police Constable Michael Caledon picked his way gingerly around the piles of gravel and dirt and dust-covered debris strewn about by the road repair crew. Buffing his black shoes to the proper wattage each morning was his least favorite activity and he had no intention of wasting the effort in his first call of the day. He'd parked the patrol car farther away than necessary for the same reason: to keep it clean.

When the road crew started up at— he looked at his watch—seven o'clock, only nine minutes away, there would be plenty of dirt and noise. He'd seen this bunch move in yesterday to rip up the street.

So complete was his concentration that he found himself on the little flagstone walk at 13 Humberview before he realized it. That surprise, coupled with his sudden awareness that the old lady was sitting on the porch waiting for him, must have showed on his face for Mrs. Van Nough explained very sweetly: "I always have my coffee on the porch in this nice weather. Sometimes I even get out before the sun is over those trees. We'll have to go inside today though; there's not much point in being out here when they start." She waved at the silent machinery on the street. "What do you take in your coffee, young man?"

Michael used the three short strides up the walk to gather himself.

"Good morning." He held out his hands. "I'm here to get . . ."

"What do you take in your coffee? I have some muffins too, that my neighbor made."

Michael didn't drink coffee, but how did he say no to such a nice old lady?

"Uh . . . just half a cup, please, and milk, lots of milk." That was how.

"Excuse me, then. I'll be right back." Mrs. Van Nough got up, shuffled over to the screen door and went inside.

Michael was having real trouble controlling his surprise. The lady was not behaving at all like a bereaved widow. Four days earlier, in fact just at this time—his watch now said 6:54—her husband had been shot in their bed. He was also surprised by how well she spoke.

Mrs. Van Nough was deaf, at least according to Sergeant Cosman. Michael had been sent because he was the best on the force at sign language. So far that skill seemed entirely superfluous.

His surprise was not diminished in the least when Mrs. Van Nough came back out the door saying: "No doubt you're wondering how we're able to communicate so easily? Well, I wasn't always deaf. Not until my accident four years ago. Here's your coffee, Constable. I can sign. Are you the one they said would come because you can sign? There's not much need. I'm pretty good at lips. You get good. You have to. Besides, everybody always says the same things to old ladies anyway!"

Her smile grew even sweeter. Michael was so charmed he was almost able to ignore the taste of coffee.

"My other little trick," she lowered her voice conspiratorially, "now don't you tell anybody, Constable." Her smile grew wider and even more irresistible. "My other little trick is, I do all the talking! People don't mind if old ladies prattle on, now do they?

Now you want to know all about poor Alvin, don't you? I don't know why. I told those other nice policemen everything. Poor Alvin. We were only married three years, you see. He was my third husband."

Without realizing it, Michael bit into a second muffin. He didn't say a word as Mrs. Van Nough continued. "It happened when I was having my coffee here, just like this. It was a beautiful day, one of those extra-special summer days. You know, clear, warm. Of course I didn't hear the shot, so poor Alvin . . ."

With a raucous cough, the first of the diesel engines started out on the street, followed by another, then a third, filling the air with aggressive clatter. The operators held the throttles open, not just to warm up their machines, but also to ensure that everyone in hearing distance would be awake to appreciate their efforts.

Mrs. Van Nough winced. The early morning breeze had brought the exhaust fumes onto the porch.

"Come," she shouted over the din. "We'll go inside. Would you carry the muffins?"

Michael picked up the plate and followed her. How, he thought to himself, how on earth am I going to tell Sergeant Cosman that such a sweet old lady is a liar?

What has tipped Michael Caledon to the realization that Mrs. Van Nough may not be all she pretends?

SOLUTION:

A deaf person would not react to ambient noise by raising her voice to compensate for it. Quite likely, Mrs. Van Nough can hear, and if so, would find it difficult to explain why she did not hear the gunshot that killed poor Alvin while she was supposedly on the porch.

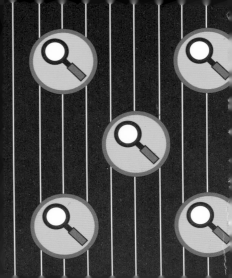